To my parents
KH
For my niece Charlotte
JW

A TEMPLAR BOOK

First published in the UK in 2016 by Templar Publishing,
part of the Bonnier Publishing Group,
The Plaza, 535 King's Road, London, SW10 0SZ
www.templarco.co.uk
www.bonnierpublishing.com

Illustrations copyright © 2016 by Jo Williamson

1 3 5 7 9 10 8 6 4 2

ISBN 978-1-8370-383-8 Hardback
ISBN 978-1-8370-490-3 Paperback

Designed by Genevieve Webster
Edited by Alison Ritchie

Printed in China

Petunia Paris's Parrot

Written by Katie Haworth & illustrated by Jo Williamson

templar publishing

Every year before Petunia Paris's birthday,
Petunia's parents asked her what present she would like.

Her fifth birthday was no different.
Petunia Paris thought. And thought. And thought.

She already had a swimming pool.
That was last year's present.

She already had a city of toys.
That was from the year before.

She also had a thousand dresses, her own personal library and
a bicycle with its own chauffeur.

Petunia couldn't think of a single thing she wanted. And so she said
the first thing that popped into her head.
"I would like a parrot please, most perfectest Mummy and Daddy."

So Petunia's parents organised the usual birthday party . . .

. . . which was splendid, of course . . .

. . . and her present was given to her with a flourish.

It was a beautiful scarlet macaw all the way from Peru.

Petunia was pleased with her parrot.

She had heard that parrots were great conversationalists so as soon as
the last guests had gone home, Petunia stood and waited for it to speak.

But all it said was "squarrk".

It was not a pretty sound.

It was NOT a promising start.

But Petunia Paris was an extremely determined young lady
and so she decided to persevere.
She tried plying him with exotic food . . .

. . . playing him the piano . . .

. . . and planning preposterous new outfits for him.

But none of Petunia's ploys prevailed.

And the only thing her parrot said was:

Squarrk

After months of trying her best to make her parrot talk,
persistent Petunia finally lost her composure:

"Excuse me," said the butler, "might I make a suggestion? Suppose you try asking him nicely, Miss Paris?"

So Petunia politely enquired, "Please, Mr Parrot, I was wondering if you would be so kind as to tell me why you won't speak to me? Is there something wrong?"

And it was then that the parrot spoke . . .

"I DO NOT WANT
a perfectly presented pile of prawns.

I DO NOT WANT
a pleasantly played piano solo.

I DO NOT WANT
to ponder parrot philosophy.

I DO NOT WANT
to wear a pink parrot poncho.

I DO NOT WANT ANY of it, Petunia Paris!"

Petunia Paris was rather perturbed.

But she still had the presence of mind to ask him one more question:

And Petunia Paris's parrot said very softly:

Every year before Petunia Paris's birthday, Petunia's parents asked her what present she would like. Her sixth birthday was no different.

This time Petunia Paris did not need to think at all.

"Can we go to Peru please, most perfectest Mummy and Daddy?"

It was a very long journey to Peru
but Petunia Paris's parrot did not stop
talking the whole way there.

And Petunia Paris's sixth birthday party was very different
from any she'd had before.